Ten
Flashing
Fireflies

By Philemon Sturges
Illustrated by
Anna Vojtech

North-South Books / New York / London

Text copyright © 1995 by Philemon Sturges
Illustrations copyright © 1995 by Anna Vojtech

All rights reserved. No part of this book may be reproduced
or utilized in any form or by any means, electronic or mechanical,
including photocopying, recording, or any information storage
and retrieval system, without permission in writing from the publisher.

Published in the United States by North-South Books Inc., New York.

Published simultaneously in Great Britain, Canada, Australia,
and New Zealand in 1995 by North-South Books, an imprint of
Nord-Süd Verlag AG, Gossau Zürich, Switzerland.

Library of Congress Cataloging-in-Publication Data is available.
A CIP catalogue record for this book is available from The British Library.
ISBN 1-55858-420-X (trade edition) 10 9 8 7 6 5 4 3 2 1
ISBN 1-55858-421-8 (library edition) 10 9 8 7 6 5 4 3 2 1

Typography by Marc Cheshire
Printed in Belgium

What do we see in the summer night?
Ten flashing fireflies burning bright!
Catch the one twinkling there
Like a star.

One flashing firefly in our jar.

What do we see in the summer night?
Nine flashing fireflies burning bright!
Capture another one.
Now there are

Two flashing fireflies in our jar.

What do we see in the summer night?
Eight twinkling fireflies blinking bright!
Let's catch another one.
Now there are

Three twinkling fireflies in our jar.

What do we see in the summer night?
Seven bright fireflies. What a sight!
Catch the one by the bush.
Now there are

Four flickering fireflies in our jar.

What do we see in the summer night?
Six sparkling fireflies blinking bright.
Catch the one flying high.
Now there are

Five fiery fireflies in our jar.

What do we see in the summer night?
Five fiery fireflies flashing bright.
Get the one way up there.
Now there are

Six sparking fireflies in our jar.

What do we see in the summer night?
Four flickering fireflies' flashing light.
You've caught another one.
Now there are

Seven bright fireflies in our jar.

What do we see in the starry night?
Three twinkling fireflies' glowing light.
I've caught another one.
Now there are

Eight twinkling fireflies in our jar.

What do we see in this dark blue night?
Two flashing fireflies' golden light.
We've caught another one.
Now there are

Nine flashing fireflies in our jar.

What do we see in this dark, dark night?
One flashing firefly's lonely light.
I'm glad we caught it—
For now there are

Ten flashing fireflies in our jar.

Let's go to bed by the jar's bright light.
Pull up the covers and say good night.
Watch them all carefully,
Look, they are

Blinking so slowly in our jar.

Open the jar, for it's much more fun,
Watching them fly away, one by one.
Fly out the window and flash good-bye.
Fly away, fly away, fly, firefly.

Ten, nine, eight, seven, six, five, four, three, two, one

Dash away, flash away.
Now there are none.